Presented to the children of

St Mary Magdalen's Catholic Primary School

by

Mr J.F. Murphy

Headteacher 1999 - 2004

*F*OR PETER AND PETER
B.D.

*F*OR ROSEMARY, MY PARENTS
AND EVERYONE AT WALKER BOOKS
I.A.

First published 1998 by Walker Books Ltd
87 Vauxhall Walk, London SE11 5HJ

This edition published 1999

2 4 6 8 10 9 7 5 3 1

Text © 1998 Berlie Doherty
Illustrations © 1998 Ian Andrew

The right of Berlie Doherty to be identified as author
of this work has been asserted by her in accordance
with the Copyright, Designs and Patents Act 1988.

This book has been typeset in Tiepolo Bold.

Printed in Hong Kong

British Library Cataloguing in Publication Data
A catalogue record for this book is
available from the British Library.

ISBN 0-7445-6067-2

The Midnight Man

BERLIE DOHERTY

ILLUSTRATED BY **IAN ANDREW**

WALKER BOOKS
AND SUBSIDIARIES
LONDON • BOSTON • SYDNEY

Every night, when Harry and Mister Dog
are asleep, someone comes riding by.

Mister Dog opens one eye and grunts.

Harry opens one eye and yawns.

They both sit up

and gaze out of the window,

and this is what they see...

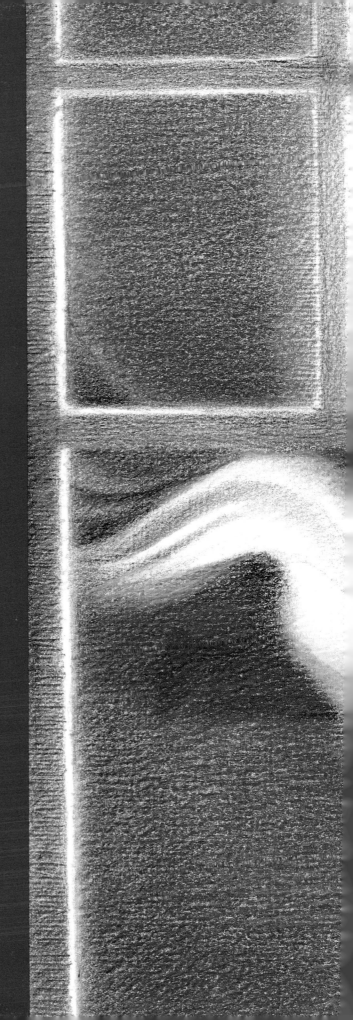

The midnight man comes
riding through the town
on his midnight horse
with its hushing hooves.
His cloak of whispers
swirls around like sighs.
On his hip is a sack of stars.

He pauses, and his horse nods its head and waits.
Then he flings the stars far up to the deep dark sky
and there they hang and glitter like flowers of ice.

And some come sprinkling over Mister Dog,

round his nose, and make him sneeze.

And some brush against Harry's face and dust his eyes.

"Who is it?" whispers Harry.

"Woof!" woofs Mister Dog.

 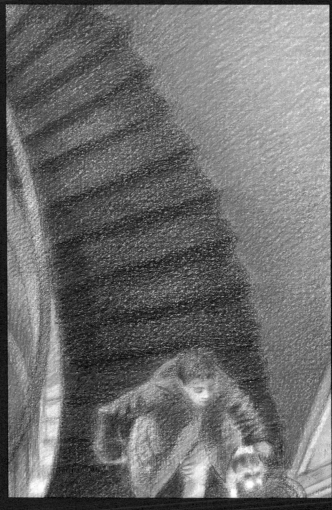

They tiptoe downstairs, past all the snoring doors,
and they're out and up the street
before the latch clicks shut.

The midnight man goes riding on his midnight horse
and all the black shadow-cats slink around
his midnight-quiet hooves.

"Wait for me!" Harry shouts, but his voice is soft as mist
and his feet make sounds like hushes on the ground.
"Woof!" woofs Mister Dog,
but his woof has turned to shush
and his paws are faint as feathers
as he trots along behind.

"You can't come with me!" the midnight man laughs.

His voice is like owl-cries and fox-calls far away.

"I have the world to travel.

There's no resting-place for me."

But still they call, and still they run,
and still they make no sound ...
down the streets and over bridges,
under arches, through the trees,

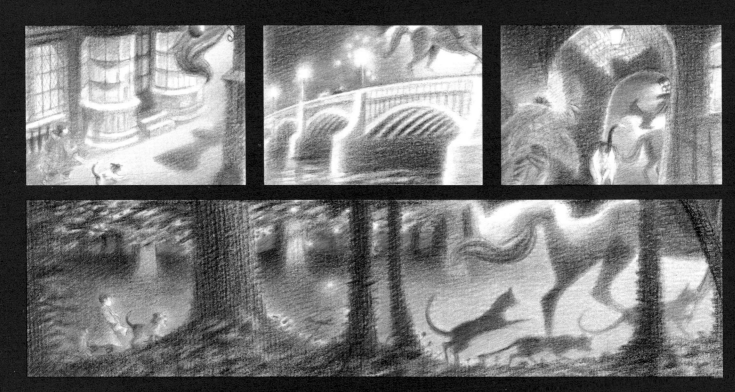

till they come to the last house
at the very end of town
where the moors stretch into darkness
as if there's no world left.

And softer and fainter go the pittering midnight hooves.

"No resting-place for me. My home is midnight land."

The midnight man turns once ...

and once he waves his hand.

Harry and Mister Dog lie sleeping on the ground

where the moors stretch away to the end of the world.

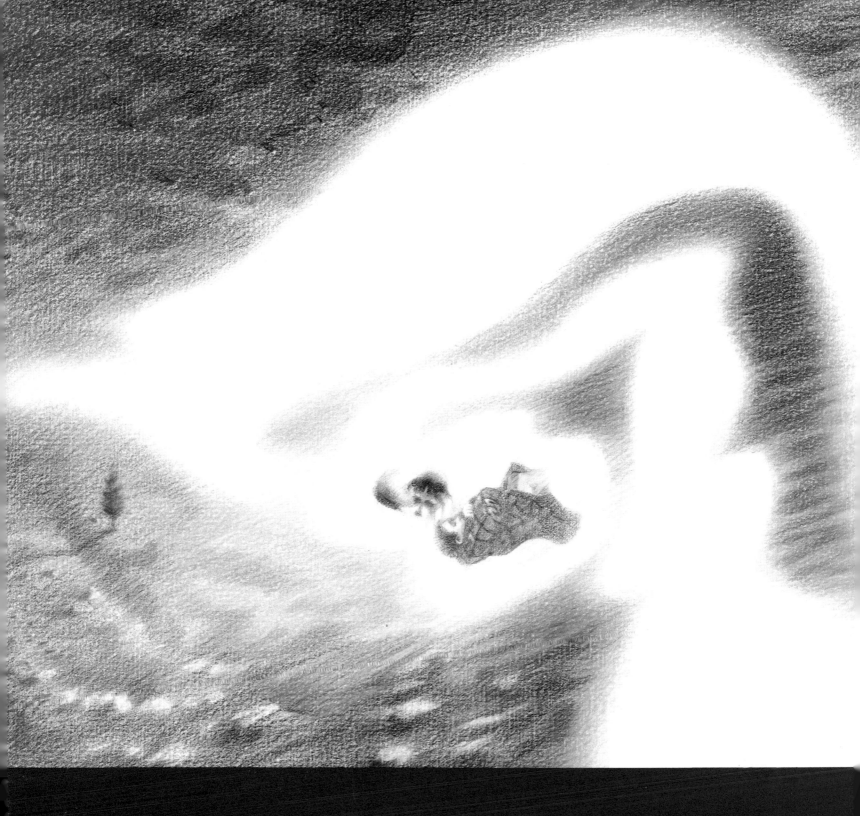

But the white moon sees as she swings across the sky.

She slides down the darkness and peers at them and cries.

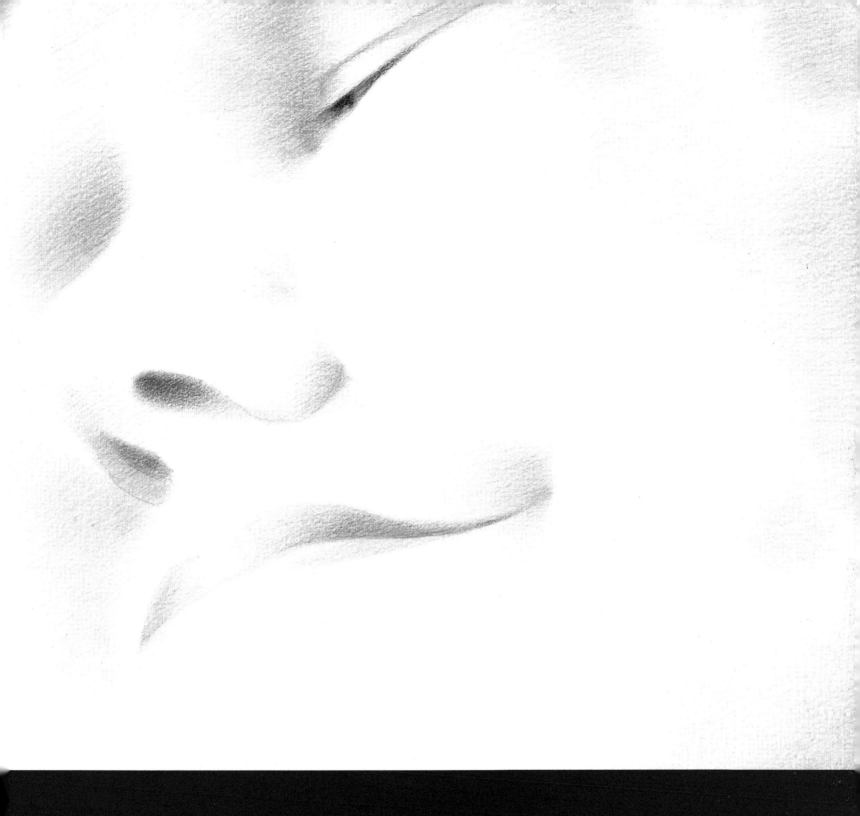

She cradles them into her creamy arms and sways back
through the trees where the midnight man had been...

Under arches, over bridges, down the streets,
past the slinking shadow-cats
to the door of Harry's house,
with the latch clicked shut.

She streams through the window,
and glides up the tiptoe stairs
and folds them down
into their tousled beds.

Mister Dog opens one eye and grunts.

Harry opens one eye and yawns.

They seem to see a winking moon

slipping through the starry sky.

They seem to hear a midnight horse

galloping on midnight hooves.

And do they hear a midnight voice,

laughing like owl-cries and fox-calls,

from far across the world...

"Midnight man!" says Harry.

"Woof!" woofs Mister Dog.

They brush the star dust from their eyes
and sleep till morning comes.

MORE WALKER PAPERBACKS
For You to Enjoy

CATKIN
by Antonia Barber/P.J. Lynch

Shortlisted for the Kate Greenaway Medal and Winner of the
Bisto Irish Children's Book Award (Illustrator Category)

The enchanting story of a tiny cat called Catkin sent to bring back a human child
from the magical Little People, who have taken her for their own.

"Barber is a superb storyteller and this tale … has the captivating quality of a
fairy story handed down through generations. Richly illustrated by
P.J. Lynch it is a joy to read aloud." *The Daily Telegraph*

0-7445-4768-7   £5.99

KATE'S GIANTS
by Valiska Gregory/Virginia Austin

Kate doesn't like the attic door in her room. Scary things might come
through it, she thinks. There might be wild animals or giants…

"This book with its warm and intimate illustrations and reassuring text shows
how the power of imagination can be used to control
fear as well as provoking it." *Baby Magazine*

0-7445-4069-0   £4.99

IN THE MIDDLE OF THE NIGHT
by Kathy Henderson/Jennifer Eachus

While one world sleeps, another comes to life – the world of nightworkers
in the city: nurses, bakers, cleaners, mail-sorters…

"A great picture book, lovely." *Chris Powling, BBC Radio*

0-7445-3143-8   £4.99

Walker Paperbacks are available from most booksellers, or by post from B.B.C.S., P.O. Box 941, Hull, North Humberside HU1 3YQ
24 hour telephone credit card line 01482 224626

To order, send: Title, author, ISBN number and price for each book ordered, your full name and address,
cheque or postal order payable to BBCS for the total amount and allow the following for postage and packing:
UK and BFPO: £1.00 for the first book, and 50p for each additional book to a maximum of £3.50.
Overseas and Eire: £2.00 for the first book, £1.00 for the second and 50p for each additional book.

Prices and availability are subject to change without notice.